Querido dragón va a la estación de bomberos

Dear Dragon Goes to the Firehouse

por/by Margaret Hillert

ilustrado por/Illustrated by David Schimmell

NORWOOD HOUSE PRESS

Queridos padres y maestros:

La serie para lectores principiantes es una colección de lecturas cuidadosamente escritas, muchas de las cuales ustedes recordarán de su propia infancia. Cada libro comprende palabras de uso frecuente en español e inglés y, a través de la repetición, le ofrece al niño la oportunidad de practicarlas. Los detalles adicionales de las ilustraciones refuerzan la historia y le brindan la oportunidad de ayudar a su niño a desarrollar el lenguaje oral y la comprensión.

Primero, léale el cuento al niño; después deje que él lea las palabras con las que está familiarizado y pronto, podrá leer solito todo el cuento. En cada paso, elogie el esfuerzo del niño para que se sienta más confiado como lector independiente. Hable sobre las ilustraciones y anime al niño a relacionar el cuento con su propia vida.

Sobre todo, la parte más importante de la experiencia de la lectura es ¡divertirse y disfrutarla!

Shannon Cannon

Shannon Cannon
Consultora de lectoescritura

Dear Caregiver,

The *Beginning-to-Read* series is a carefully written collection of readers, many of which you may remember from your own childhood. This book, *Dear Dragon's Day with Father*, was written over 30 years after the first *Dear Dragon* books were published. The *New Dear Dragon* series features the same elements of the earlier books, such as text comprised of common sight words. These sight words provide your child with ample practice reading the words that appear most frequently in written text. The many additional details in the pictures enhance the story and offer the opportunity for you to help your child expand oral language skills and develop comprehension.

Begin by reading the story to your child, followed by letting him or her read familiar words and soon your child will be able to read the story independently. At each step of the way, be sure to praise your reader's efforts to build his or her confidence as an independent reader. Discuss the pictures and encourage your child to make connections between the story and his or her own life.

Above all, the most important part of the reading experience is to have fun and enjoy it!

Shannon Cannon,
Literacy Consultant

Norwood House Press • P.O. Box 316598 • Chicago, Illinois 60631
For more information about Norwood House Press please visit our website at *www.norwoodhousepress.com* or call 866-565-2900.

Special thanks to Gayle Vaul-Kennedy of the Chicago Fire Department.

LIBRARY OF CONGRESS CATALOGING-IN-PUBLICATION DATA
Hillert, Margaret.
  [Dear dragon goes to the firehouse. Spanish & English]
  Querido dragón va a la estación de bomberos = Dear dragon goes to the firehouse / por/by Margaret Hillert ; ilustrado por/illustrated by David Schimmell ; [translated by Eida del Risco].
    p. cm. -- (A beginning-to-read book)
  Includes word list.
  Summary: "A boy and his pet dragon go on a class trip to the local firehouse and learn about what it takes to put out a fire. Carefully translated to include English and Spanish text"-- Provided by publisher.
  ISBN-13: 978-1-59953-468-8 (library edition : alk. paper)
  ISBN-10: 1-59953-468-1 (library edition : alk. paper)
[1. Fire departments--Fiction. 2. Dragons--Fiction. 3. Spanish language materials--Bilingual.] I. Schimmell, David, ill. II. Del Risco, Eida. III. Title. IV. Title: Dear dragon goes to the firehouse.
  PZ73.H557211 2011
  [E]--dc23

                          2011016649

Manufactured in the United States of America in North Mankato, Minnesota.
178N—072011

Es un buen día para dar un paseo.
Vamos de paseo y...
¿a que no adivinan?

It is a good day for a walk.
We will go for a walk and—
Guess what?

3

Vamos a ver algo grande.
Una cosa grande que nos presta ayuda.

We will see something big.
A big thing that is a good help to us.

Vamos.
Vamos a caminar y a caminar.
Caminar nos hace bien.

Here we go.
We will walk
     and walk and walk.
A walk is good for us.

5

Miren allá arriba.
Está en rojo así que tenemos que PARAR.

Look up there.
It is red so we have to STOP.

6

Ahora está en VERDE.
Podemos PASAR.
Vamos. Vamos.

Now it is GREEN.
So we can GO, GO, GO.
Come on. Come on.

7

Ya llegamos.
Este es la estación de bomberos.

Here we are.
This is the firehouse.

Oooh.
Miren eso.
Qué grande. Qué GRANDE.

O-o-o-h—
Look at that.
So big. So BIG.

Sí, es grande.
Y nos presta ayuda.

Yes, it is.
And it is a big help to us.

Entren. Entren.
Nos alegra verlos.

Come in. Come in.
We are happy to see you.

Cuando vamos a un fuego,
nos ponemos esto
        y esto
              y esto.

When we go to a fire we
put on this—
        and this—
              and this.

Y para apagar el fuego,
tenemos que tener esto
    y esto
       y esto.

And to help us put out a fire,
we have to have this—
    and this—
       and this.

Eh, mira el perro.
¿Es un perro bombero?
¿Verdad?

Oh, look at the dog.
Is it a fire dog?
Is it?

No. Es un amigo.
Él no trabaja.
Le gusta estar aquí.
Le damos de comer.

No. He is a friend.
He does not work.
He likes it here.
We give him things to eat.

Ponte esto.
A ver cómo luces.

Put this on.
See how you look.

Ay, no.
No me sirve.
Me queda demasiado grande.

Oh, no.
This is not good.
It is too big for me.

Tengo algo para ustedes.
Uno para ti
    y para ti
        y para ti.

I have something for you.
One for you—
    and you—
        and you.

Mapa de la ciudad
City Map

Calle Roble = Oak St.
Calle Segunda = Second St.
Orilla = Riverside
Calle Tercera = Third St.
Calle Cerezo = Cherry St.
Calle Primera = First St.
Estación de Bomberos
Fire Station
Calle Nogal = Walnut St.

¡Ooooh!
Cascos de bombero.
Cascos de bombero rojos.

Ooooooh!
Fire hats.
Red fire hats.

Y algo para mirar.
¡Mira este libro!

And something to look at.
Look at this book!

No juegues con fuego.

Do not play with fire.

Es muy grande y rojo.
¿Podemos subir?

This is so big and red.
Can we go up there?

23

Sí. Sí.
Suban.
¡Arriba! ¡Arriba!

Yes. Yes.
Go up.
Up, Up, Up!

25

Ahora nos tenemos que ir.
Fue divertido estar aquí.
Pero ahora nos
    tenemos que ir.

Now we have to go.
It was fun to be here.
But now we
    have to go.

27

Yo estoy contigo
y tú estás conmigo.
Qué divertido.
Qué divertido, querido dragón.

Here I am with you.
And here you are with me.
What fun.
What fun, dear dragon.

The following activities support the findings of the National Reading Panel that determined the most effective components for reading instruction are: Phonemic Awareness, Phonics, Vocabulary, Fluency, and Text Comprehension.

Phonemic Awareness: The /o/ sound

Sound Substitution: Say the following words to your child and ask him or her to substitute the middle sound in the word with /o/:

tip = top	seed = sod	luck = lock	jig = jog
sick = sock	leg = log	step = stop	ship = shop
pat = pot	dill = doll	let = lot	rib = rob
fix = fox	tick = tock	deck = dock	

Phonics: The letters O and o

1. Demonstrate how to form the letters **O** and **o** for your child.

2. Have your child practice writing **O** and **o** at least three times each.

3. Write down the following letters and spaces and ask your child to write the letter **o** on the spaces in each word:

bl_ck	st_p	m_m	m_p	j_b
d_t	t_p	sh_p	cl_ck	dr_p
fr_g	tr_t	h_t	l_g	kn_ck
n_t	s_ck	g_t		

Vocabulary: Concept Words

1. Write the following words on separate pieces of paper and point to them as you read them to your child:

truck	hose	firefighter
boots	helmet	flames

2. Say the following sentences aloud and ask your child to point to the word that is described:

- This is a person who puts out fires. (firefighter)
- Firefighters wear these to keep their feet and legs safe. (boots)
- This is what firefighters wear to protect their heads. (helmet)
- Firefighters ride on this to get to the fire. (truck)
- The fire truck has a very big one of these to get water to the fire. (hose)
- The hose helps firefighters put these out. (flames)

Fluency: Shared Reading/CLOZE

1. Reread the story with your child at least two more times while your child tracks the print by running a finger under the words as they are read. Ask your child to read the words he or she knows with you.

2. Reread the story, stopping occasionally so your child can supply the next word. For example, *We will see something _____* (big), or *It is red so we have to _____* (stop), or *Do not play with _____* (fire).

3. Now have your child reread the story, stopping occasionally for you to supply the next word.

Text Comprehension: Discussion Time

1. Ask your child to retell the sequence of events in the story.

2. To check comprehension, ask your child the following questions:

- What color on the light means it is safe to walk?
- What do firefighters wear? Why?
- Why did Dear Dragon laugh at the boy?
- What did the firefighter give the kids?

Photograph by Glenna Washburn

ACERCA DE LA AUTORA Margaret Hillert ha escrito más de 80 libros para niños que están aprendiendo a leer. Sus libros han sido traducidos a muchos idiomas y han sido leídos por más de un millón de niños de todo el mundo. De niña, Margaret empezó escribiendo poesía y más adelante siguió escribiendo para niños y adultos. Durante 34 años, fue maestra de primer grado. Ya se retiró, y ahora vive en Michigan donde le gusta escribir, dar paseos matinales y cuidar a sus tres gatos.

ABOUT THE AUTHOR Margaret Hillert has written over 80 books for children who are just learning to read. Her books have been translated into many different languages and over a million children throughout the world have read her books. She first started writing poetry as a child and has continued to write for children and adults throughout her life. A first grade teacher for 34 years, Margaret is now retired from teaching and lives in Michigan where she likes to write, take walks in the morning, and care for her three cats.

ACERCA DEL ILUSTRADOR David Schimmell fue bombero durante 23 años, al cabo de los cuales guardó las botas y el casco y se dedicó a trabajar como ilustrador. David ha creado las ilustraciones para la nueva serie de Querido dragón, así como para muchos otros libros. David nació y se crió en Evansville, Indiana, donde aún vive con su esposa, dos hijos, un nieto y dos nietas.

ABOUT THE ILLUSTRATOR David Schimmell served as a professional firefighter for 23 years before hanging up his boots and helmet to devote himself to work as an illustrator. David has happily created the illustrations for the New Dear Dragon books as well as many other books throughout his career. Born and raised in Evansville, Indiana, he lives there today with his wife, two sons, a grandson and two granddaughters.